THE TALE OF
TOM KITTEN

BY
BEATRIX POTTER

A LITTLE SIMON BOOK

Published by Simon & Schuster, Inc.
New York

The Tale of Peter Rabbit
The Tale of Squirrel Nutkin
The Tale of Benjamin Bunny
The Tale of Tom Kitten
The Tale of Mrs. Tiggy-Winkle
The Tale of Jemima Puddle-Duck
The Tale of the Flopsy Bunnies
The Tailor of Gloucester

Created and manufactured by arrangement with Ottenheimer Publishers, Inc.

Published by LITTLE SIMON, a division of Simon & Schuster, Inc., Simon & Schuster Building, 1230 Avenue of the Americas, New York, New York 10020, by arrangement with Ottenheimer Publishers, Inc.

Printed under license from Frederick Warne & Co.

Little Simon and colophon are trademarks of Simon & Schuster, Inc.

Printed in Italy.

10 9 8 7 6 5 4 3 2 1

ISBN: 0-671-62927-1

DEDICATED

TO ALL

PICKLES,

——ESPECIALLY TO THOSE THAT

GET UPON MY GARDEN WALL

ONCE upon a time there were three little kittens, and their names were Mittens, Tom Kitten, and Moppet.

They had dear little fur coats of their own; and they tumbled about the doorstep and played in the dust.

BUT one day their mother—
Mrs. Tabitha Twitchit—
expected friends to tea; so she
fetched the kittens indoors, to
wash and dress them, before
the fine company arrived.

11

FIRST she scrubbed their faces (this one is Moppet).

THEN she brushed their fur, (this one is Mittens).

15

THEN she combed their tails and whiskers (this is Tom Kitten).

Tom was very naughty, and he scratched.

MRS. TABITHA dressed
Moppet and Mittens in
clean pinafores and tuckers;
and then she took all sorts of
elegant uncomfortable clothes
out of a chest of drawers, in
order to dress up her son
Thomas.

TOM KITTEN was very fat, and he had grown; several buttons burst off. His mother sewed them on again.

WHEN the three kittens were ready, Mrs. Tabitha unwisely turned them out into the garden, to be out of the way while she made hot buttered toast.

"Now keep your frocks clean, children! You must walk on your hind legs. Keep away from the dirty ash-pit, and from Sally Henny Penny, and from the pig-stye and the Puddle-Ducks."

MOPPET and Mittens walked down the garden path unsteadily. Presently they trod upon their pinafores and fell on their noses.

When they stood up there were several green smears!

"LET us climb up the rockery, and sit on the garden wall," said Moppet.

They turned their pinafores back to front, and went up with a skip and a jump; Moppet's white tucker fell down into the road.

TOM KITTEN was quite unable to jump when walking upon his hind legs in trousers. He came up the rockery by degrees, breaking the ferns, and shedding buttons right and left.

HE was all in pieces when he reached the top of the wall.

Moppet and Mittens tried to pull him together; his hat fell off, and the rest of his buttons burst.

WHILE they were in diffi-culties, there was a pit pat paddle pat! and the three Puddle-Ducks came along the hard high road, marching one behind the other and doing the goose step—pit pat paddle pat! pit pat waddle pat!

THEY stopped and stood in a row, and stared up at the kittens. They had very small eyes and looked surprised.

THEN the two duck-birds, Rebeccah and Jemima Puddle-Duck, picked up the hat and tucker and put them on.

MITTENS laughed so that she fell off the wall. Moppet and Tom descended after her; the pinafores and all the rest of Tom's clothes came off on the way down.

"Come! Mr. Drake Puddle-Duck," said Moppet—"Come and help us to dress him! Come and button up Tom!"

MR. DRAKE PUDDLE-DUCK advanced in a slow sideways manner, and picked up the various articles.

BUT he put them on *him-self!* They fitted him even worse than Tom Kitten. "It's a very fine morning!" said Mr. Drake Puddle-Duck.

AND he and Jemima and Rebeccah Puddle-Duck set off up the road, keeping step—pit pat, paddle pat! pit pat, waddle pat!

THEN Tabitha Twitchit
came down the garden
and found her kittens on the
wall with no clothes on.

SHE pulled them off the wall, smacked them, and took them back to the house.

"My friends will arrive in a minute, and you are not fit to be seen; I am affronted," said Mrs. Tabitha Twitchit.

SHE sent them upstairs; and I am sorry to say she told her friends that they were in bed with the measles; which was not true.

QUITE the contrary; they were not in bed: *not* in the least.

Somehow there were very extraordinary noises over-head, which disturbed the dignity and repose of the tea party.

AND I think that some day
I shall have to make
another, larger, book, to tell
you more about Tom Kitten!

AS for the Puddle-Ducks—
they went into a pond.
The clothes all came off
directly, because there were
no buttons.

AND Mr. Drake Puddle-Duck, and Jemima and Rebeccah, have been looking for them ever since.